A Friend from Galilee

A Friend from Galilee

by Dandi Daley Mackall

Illustrated by Jan Spivey Gilchrist

A FRIEND FROM GALILEE

Large-quantity purchases or custom editions of this book are available at a discount from the publisher. For more information, contact the sales department at Augsburg Fortress, Publishers, 1-800-328-4648, or write to: Sales Director, Augsburg Fortress, Publishers, P.O. Box 1209, Minneapolis, MN 55440-1209.

ISBN 0-8066-4586-5

Cover and book design by Michelle L. N. Cook

The paper used in this publication meets the minimum requirements of American National Standard for Information Sciences— Permanence of Paper for Printed Library Materials, ANSI Z329.48-1984. ♾ ™

Manufactured in China

08   07   06   05   04   1   2   3   4   5   6   7   8   9   10

To Hannah,
who will always have
a Friend from Galilee
—D.D.M.

For Kendall Nichelle Rallins,
a tiny artist with tremendous talent.

Thanks to Kevin Muniz, a great model.
—J.S.G.

This book belongs to

_____

A friend of Jesus

Jesus, Jesus, growing up in Nazareth,
Living like the rest of us,
Did you sweep the floor?

Jesus, Jesus, playing down in Galilee,
Were your friends at all like me?
Was your family poor?

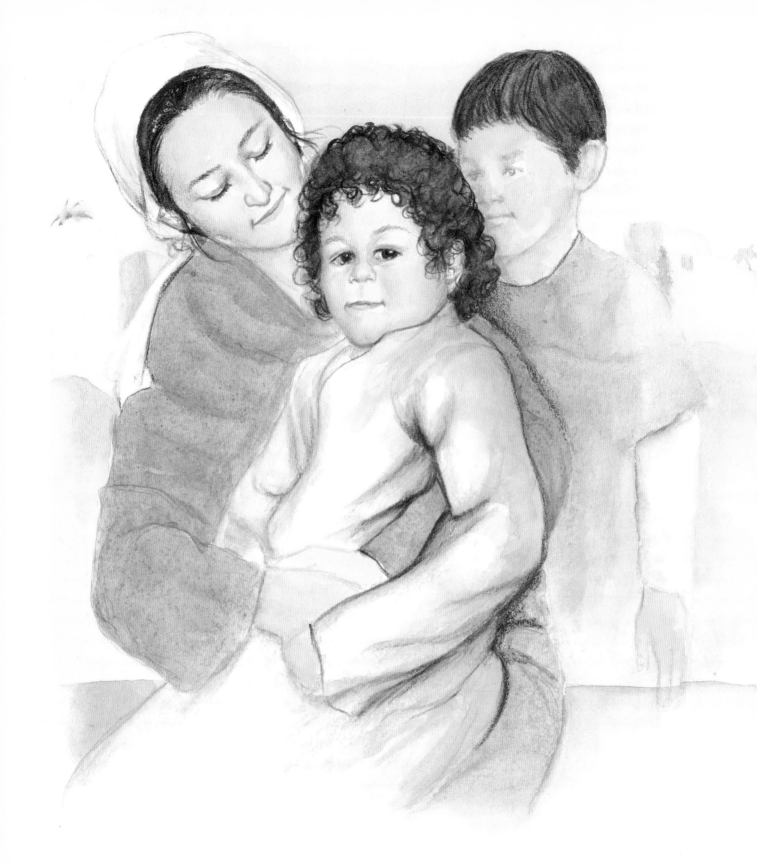

Jesus, Jesus, sitting on your mother's lap,
Did you have to take a nap?
Did she tuck you in?

Jesus, Jesus, could you make a funny face?
Did you ever run a race?
Did you like to win?

Jesus, Jesus, working in your father's shop,
Did he ever make you stop
Drawing in the dust?

Jesus, Jesus, did you have to raise your hand?
Did your teacher understand
When you disagreed?

Jesus, Jesus, ever watch a sparrow fall?
When you heard your father call,
Did you always come?

Jesus, Jesus, did you like to sing a song?
Ever get the lyrics wrong?
Did you like to hum?

Jesus, Jesus, chasing down a buzzing bee,
Did you like to climb a tree
Way out on a limb?

Jesus, Jesus, did you ever once forget?
Did you ever get upset
Doing all your chores?

Jesus, Jesus, springtime when the seeds were sown,
Did you walk the hills alone?
Plant a mustard seed?

Jesus, Jesus, did a best friend turn away?
Let you down? Refuse to play?
Did you wonder why?

Jesus, Jesus, growing up in Galilee,
Watching, waiting patiently,
Sitting on a hill.

Jesus, Jesus, did you see the things I see?
Did you want a friend like me?
Do you want one still?

Toward a Deeper Friendship

Jesus invites our questions. He asks us to seek, and he promises that we will find.
The Bible gives us an intimate portrait of Christ,
who longs for our friendship as we long for his.

Greater love has no one than this,
that one lay down his life for his friends.
You are my friends if you do what I command.
I no longer call you servants,
because a servant does not know his master's business.
Instead, I have called you friends,
for everything that I learned from my Father
I have made known to you.

— John 15:13-15, NIV

Here are some related Scripture references for families to explore together in the journey to a deeper friendship with Jesus:

Pages 8-9
Childhood—Luke 2:39-40
Home—Matthew 8:20
Friends—John 15:14-17

Pages 10-11
Mother's care—Luke 2:6-7; Luke 2:51
Nap—Matthew 8:23-24
Growing—Luke 2:52

Pages 12-13
Obedience—Luke 2:51; Matthew 15:4
Carpenter—Mark 6:1-3
Bread—Matthew 4:3-4; Matthew 6:11;
    Matthew 14:13-21; Matthew 26:26
Drawing in the dust—John 8:1-11

Pages 14-15
Physical needs—Luke 4:1-12
Stormy night—Mark 4:35-41
Light—Mark 4:21-23; John 8:12

Pages 16-17
School and teachers—Luke 2:41-50; Matthew 7:28-29
Rules—Mark 7:6-13; Matthew 12:1-14
Reads—Luke 4:14-22

Pages 18-19
Sparrow—Matthew 10:29
Father's call—John 10:1-18
Singing—Mark 14:26

Pages 20-21
Tree—Matthew 12:33
Jesus's friend—Luke 1:39-45;
    John 3:22-36
Water—Mark 6:45-52

Pages 22-23
Physical needs—Mark 6:30-31;
    John 4:1-32; John 19:28
Fish—Luke 5:1-11; Matthew 4:18-20;
    John 21:4-6
Prayer—Matthew 6:5-15; Matthew 7:7-12

Pages 24-25
Boat—Matthew 8:23-27
Coat—Matthew 5:40
Upset—Matthew 21:12-13; John 14:27
Chores—Luke 2:51; Matthew 3:13-17; John 15:10

Pages 26-27
Sowing seeds—Matthew 13:1-30
Mustard seed—Matthew 13:31-32
Harvest—Matthew 9:36-38
Need—Matthew 6:25-34; Matthew 6:19-21

Pages 28-29
Star—John 1:1-5; Matthew 2:1-12; Revelation 1:12-20
Mom—Luke 1:26-28; Luke 1:46-55
Dad—John 1:14-18; John 17:1-5
Alone—Mark 1:12; Mark 15:33-34

Pages 30-31
Road—Matthew 7:13-14
Rooster—John 13:36-38; Matthew 26:69-75
Another mile—Matthew 5:41-42
Serve—Matthew 20:16-28; John 13:1-17; Mark 10:35-45

Pages 32-33
Bullies—Matthew 12:13-14; Mark 5:17;
    Mark 6:1-6; Luke 4:28-30; Matthew 20:17-19
Mocking—Mark 5:37-43; Mark 6:1-5; Matthew 5:11-12;
    John 8:39-46; Matthew 26:67-68; Matthew 27:38-44

Pages 34-35
Prayers—Matthew 7:7-11; Luke 4:42; Matthew 26:36-46
Cares—John 15:18-27; Matthew 6:25-34
Cry—Matthew 5:3-4; Luke 6:20-23; Matthew 14:10-13;
    John 11:21-46; Matthew 23:37
Betrayed—Matthew 26:1-5; Matthew 26:14-16;
    John 13:21; John 18:12-27

Pages 36-37
Heaven—Matthew 18:1-6; Matthew 18:19-20;
    Matthew 19:13-15
Friend—John 15:12-17